DARK MAGIC
ON THE
Edge of Town

Paul Edward Costa

Paperback-Press
an imprint of A & S Publishing
A & S Holmes, Inc.

ISBN 10: 1-945669-21-7
ISBN-13: 978-1-945669-21-7

CHAPTER I

"...We didn't dare reanimate physical matter after we discovered the secret to resurrection, so we turned to the memories lost in our heads instead, from which we believed we were safe, until we brought the terror of 'The Singular Revelation' upon our thoughts and minds..."

***

Floodlights burst on and spread waves of fluorescent light over the Griega Cemetery. Tombstones of various sizes cast their shadows over the ground like stationary sundials. Coloured cloth rectangles lay on the grassy earth in front of each tombstone. Black candles stood limp, folded over, and unlit on the graves. A wooden fence made from nailed-together boards lined the cemetery's perimeter. The ground rolled along unevenly under the evening's mists.

Spotlights lit up the outside of the nearby town's stone walls at night. Their bright gray illumination matched that of the moon in the sky. Dark blue clouds found form as they floated across its hazy light before they passed on into the sky's vacuous, black abyss.

The closest section of town wall stood fifty meters off from the Griega cemetery. Risers had been erected on the wall, and silent people of all ages and genders sat patiently on their three levels while waiting for the match to begin. They wore old, worn out, but still dignified clothing, and held up intricately sewn flags attached to the tops of broom handles. Each flag consisted of two colours. Each pair of colours represented a different city district. The cloth cut outs of specific family crests had been stitched onto each flag. An ice wolf on a shield lay over a black and white flag, a bear between two leaves lay over a green and gray flag, and so on.

Two collapsed scissor lifts stood opposite each other, one at either end of the graveyard. The crowd on the town wall only murmured when they noticed the figures they saw standing on the scissor lift platforms. The lifts activated and extended up through the air, bringing the two figures across from each other into the glow of the floodlights.

A man with blue-tinted lips, a buzz cut, a large beard, and a black turtleneck/suit jacket combination stood on one lift.

An elderly man with reading glasses stood on the other. He wore a wide brimmed leather hat and an air filtration mask over his mouth and nose. He wore black dress pants and a white dress shirt with its collar open.

Both men turned to the audience on the town wall and bowed. The spectators clapped respectfully.

The Necromancers atop the scissor lifts turned and faced each other across the Griega cemetery. They began their opening rituals.

They raised the long steel wands they held, which grew hot, but the men's hands—with scarred, disfigured palms—stayed steady. They waved their arms in front of them according to detailed formations they'd long since memorized. Prongs shaped like beastly claws held charcoal chunks in place at the ends of both wands.

A light rain began falling. The audience on the risers stayed still. They stared straight ahead and paid no attention to the raindrops collecting on their faces and rolling down over their noses and chins. The rest of the modest downpour made the ground of the Griega cemetery damp.

Corporeal figures concealed by black cloaks and dark, wide-brimmed hats began appearing, flickering, and vanishing in the spaces between the graves like images displayed by an ancient hologram cube.

The coloured cloth rectangles lying flat before each tombstone matched the flags held by the spectators. They began levitating off the ground, billowing as if wind blew up beneath them. The flags didn't remain flat as they rose off the ground. The center of each one lifted higher than its outside edges, giving the impression that different beings stood underneath the flags. These figures thrashed about, lashing out with long arms while their heads shook violently from side to side.

The audience almost filled the first three rows of risers, except for a trio of empty spots at the far end of the third row.

Chapter II

"...We wandered inside the walls of our small town and down its narrow streets for so long after our collective, simultaneous Revelation. It made us see warm rooms as only confined, isolated cells. It made us see our city's streets as only looping paths without a destination. It made us see other wandering townsfolk as only hollow reflections of our lost selves. If someone asked 'why?' out loud, silence alone answered. Eventually–out of frustration, or simply a lack of other options–many drifted up to the city walls...."

***

Scott and Nareni left a café in the town several hours after nightfall. They continued their date night—a weekly tradition they'd kept up for forty years—with a walk along the river Lahni. The river Lahni bisected the town where they lived. A low, white-stone wall lined the river on either side. The freshly lit street lanterns immersed the city in a dark yellow glow. That same light flashed over the river's black, restless waters. Old stone buildings, tightly packed together and all under three stories in height, lined the town's winding, cobblestone streets. Dark and narrow alleys lay where these buildings occasionally didn't touch, but none knew what lay past those claustrophobic passages, in deeper sections of the city where no residents ever ventured—either in body or mind.

Scott and Nareni walked arm in arm. They kept walking until they reached one of the town's far walls just past the abandoned sugar factory. It stood like a monolith with its tall sides made of smooth, windowless, and filthy concrete. Scott wore a beige suit and a white shirt with no tie. He combed his silver hair and parted it at the side for this occasion. He held a walking stick. Nareni wore horn-rimmed glasses and a blue dress with black, solid, high-heeled shoes.

Scott and Nareni exchanged a mutual glance, smiled sadly, and turned back towards the center of the city.

They stopped briefly in a small garden consisting of flowers fashioned from rusted iron. A sign sat atop a black pole embedded in the sidewalk. It had a cracked, glass cover so coated in dust that it rendered the sign behind it barely legible, but Nareni squinted and made out the words "Echo Garden: please stop and listen".

Scott and Nareni looked at each other and held each other's hands. They shrugged and remained silent. They bent their necks at different angles, trying to pick up any sounds they could, but they only heard the river lapping against its stone sides, until another sound suddenly emerged just as they prepared to move on.

They heard a strange, arrhythmic patter behind them. Scott and Nareni kept their eyes closed, thinking of this sound as part of the installation, until it stopped when a hoarse, cracked, and monotone voice said "blood ran over the skin. It circled around the drain. Pretty swirls. Did you get what you wanted? I'm glad you did. Blood ran over the skin. It spiraled down the drain. Such pretty swirls..."

Scott let go of Nareni's hand. He turned and opened his

eyes. He flinched. A painful wince crossed his face, but he grimaced and faced what he saw in front of him.

A corpse crouched on the ground. It wore a purple velvet dress torn ragged all over. The corpse had pale skin covered by spots where its flesh had fallen away, or been eaten through by maggots. The deceased body moved with a feral crawl using only three limbs—its right arm, and both bent legs—while holding its stomach with its left hand. It had lips like an antique doll. Black, curly hair hung over most of its face, but Scott saw those same lips moving constantly, repeating its words. It jerked its head from left to right while bending its neck at odd angles when it spoke.

Scott took a step forwards.

"I never asked such a thing of you!" he said before he raised his walking stick, fully intending to drive its bottom end through the corpse's neck.

Nareni stood still. She clasped her hands in front of her and bowed her head. She kept her eyes shut and wore a neutral expression on her face, indicating only her physical presence. Her breathing quickened, but the walking stick suddenly flew out of Scott's hand. It clattered to the ground and skidded across the street's stones towards an alley between two buildings. Its wood form twisted, cracked, and split in half.

"Goodness, gracious me," said a voice from the shadows. "You have my deepest apologies for this little...slip up."

A man walked out from the dark alley. He wore a beard beginning to hang down noticeably from his jaw and buzz-cut brown hair which ended in a widow's peak on his forehead. He smiled broadly. He had skin like worn leather and piercing, blue eyes. His lips were a light shade of blue, as if cold. He wore a turtle neck, a blazer, and trousers all coloured the same shade of black. His right hand curled over the prongs atop a steel wand he leaned on like a cane.

"But if I may be so bold as to ask," he continued, "what

in heavens are you two doing all the way in here? The rest took seats on the city wall for the…festivities, though of course the first match concluded by now, but you do have time to view the remainder in store for the rest of tonight. We put on quite the show, I must say, it's a shame you missed the opening, all went splendidly, well, of course for this little specimen who got away during intermission" the man said as he gestured towards the corpse which had crept up behind Scott and Nareni.

It remained crouched on three limbs in its torn velvet dress while holding its stomach. It remained silent and still, except for its head, which continued its restless twitching and jerking as if according to a deeply internalized prayer.

"As a professional, I must assure you both that this one here is an outlier, statistically, one of the few particles that doesn't quite follow the rest when fired, that pings off on its own," the man squatted down and roughly patted the corpse's head, "that's what you are, right? An outlier, a bad apple, a toy broken in the box, not representative at all, isn't that right?!" he shoved his hand against the side of the corpse's head and sent it twitching onto its side on the sidewalk.

The man sighed. He tapped his staff against the ground and the chunk of coal atop it rattled once. Scott and Nareni blinked.

The corpse stood up straight. Milk-white pools clouded its gray, dead eyes hidden behind strands of curly, black hair. Its feet poked out from the bottom of the velvet dress. The corpse stood on its toes like a ballerina. The man in the black turtleneck grimaced and waved his hand behind him, as if saying "behold." The corpse tip-toed across the cobblestone street and into the black slit of an alley between two smoke-stained, stone buildings, into a deeper part of the city.

"I bid the both of you adieu," the man said. He smiled and the way his eyes squinted indicated that he forced the gesture. "Have a pleasant evening," he said before he turned sharply and crossed the cobblestone street. He entered the alley where the corpse had disappeared and the shadows therein absorbed his black-clad form.

Scott pinched the bridge of his nose and kept his eyes shut.

"I'm sorry, Nareni," Scott said, "but after seeing that...I need to just, sit, and get lost in the next match." Nareni looked at him. "I don't know what else will help right now. I'm going to go to the top of the wall, with the others. Will you come with me?"

Nareni said nothing and turned her head from side to side while holding her arms in the chill of the night.

Scott turned away.

"I understand," he said. "But please remain safe, wherever you go."

CHAPTER III

"...So many stood on our town's stone walls that no others could join them. So many gathered there that those of us still on the city streets longed to climb up as well. We heard our brethren on the walls shouting like a ship's captain sighting land after a long journey. We saw them raise their arms and form Y-shaped silhouettes against the sky. We next heard their feet pounding up and down, as if in frustration. They sounded like an approaching army. I threw a pebble at a townsperson on the wall to get their attention. They turned to me. I asked what they saw beyond the town walls, but the townsperson I spoke with simply hung their head and gave a half-shrug before they buried their face in their hands. One by one, like dominoes, they each toppled forward over the walls..."

***

Slav stood alone atop a long section of town wall on the opposite side of the city. Most of the town's residents were not in bed and had gathered on the risers where they witnessed the match between Necromancers unfolding on the Griega Cemetery before them.

Short, rectangular towers rose up out of the town walls at equal intervals like teeth. Slav leaned against one of these towers—most of which contained stairwells to ground level—and looked out at the land before him which he saw dimly lit by the partially obstructed moonlight. Dirt roads snaked out the city gates and down the land he saw descending into a long, flat slope. The ground contained short fruit trees and wide, thorny bushes growing out of dry dirt. Just past a short hill stood a cluster of Douglas fir trees adjacent to the small Zeta Cemetery. A short wall of stacked stones built by master masons lined the three adjacent sides of the burial site. Inside were seventy graves, each marked by slabs of engraved marble or simple tombstones sculpted from rock, all arranged in rows.

Slav wore a navy blue P-coat with its collar turned up. Small, round sunglasses with reflective, mirrored lenses rested on his nose. They covered his eyes. His wavy brown hair blew wildly about his head in the high winds atop the town walls. He kept his hands in his pockets and his mouth bore a permanent half-smile which people often interpreted as sinister or reassuring, depending on their relationship with him.

Nareni quietly emerged from the doorway of the rectangular stone tower to the right of the one on which Slav leaned. Shadows half obscured her form. The moonlight highlighted the gray strands in her black hair and the lenses of her rectangular glasses. She still wore her blue dress, but she carried her high heeled shoes. She showed no sign of finding this uncomfortable due to having already developed tough soles as a child. Slav remained still and didn't turn towards her. If he sensed her approach, he gave no indication of having done so.

Nareni looked from side to side. Upon seeing no one else with them on the wall, she said "why aren't you watching the match?"

Slav said "because they're like mechanical chess players."

Nareni nodded and walked towards Slav. She stopped next to him and waited for him to speak, but he remained silent.

"It finally happened, didn't it?" Slav said.

Nareni held her left wrist with her right hand. She walked towards the edge of the wall. "It did," she said. "In the intermission after the first match... during the walk we often take. I never thought I'd have to meet her after Scott confessed his affair to me, especially in that state of...decay..."

"There's always a few who break away from the necromancy spells, and go after their own memories."

Nareni said "I just want all of it to stop now."

"And that's why you agreed to come help after all?"

"If I do, this will stop, won't it? They won't be able to hold the matches for next year's games? If there was any other Scott was with...I can't bear them coming back, and I can't wait a whole year to find out if another will get away from the Necromancers and come for us."

Slav turned to her. "It will stop the games coming up next year, yes," he said. "My, does this mean you agree with me, at last, that the matches are abhorrent?"

"No, I can't come that far to agree with you."

"But you'll still help me stop them?"

"Not many of the resurrected get away, you know." Nareni turned to Slav. She stood slightly taller than him, even when not wearing her heels. "Do you know how damaging it is for those who have received visits? God, there's a reason the mayor only approved physical necromancy for the matches. You'd think the return visits would be wonderful, but they never are. The dead will only speak of the pain still lingering in them, the same pain the living are quick to forget, and their appearance..." Nareni shuddered. "The point is, I've forgiven Scott for his lapses, but I haven't forgotten, of course I haven't forgotten, so I don't need a reminder from a dead lover who can't let go. There may be no more in the Zeta cemetery...but if there are, I want to be sure they won't come for us...that no dead 'outliers' will come back for anyone."

"Scott's lapses? Is that what you're calling them? And it's never over, Nareni. If you have to say something's 'over', then you damn-well know it's far from ever being that."

Nareni moved closer to Slav.

"Then why bother with your plan here tonight? Hmm?" she said.

"The dead's business with us will never be 'over'; there's no way of 'sorting things out'... but we can block the path, so to speak, so the dead can't get close enough to us to voice their grievances or whatever," Slav said.

Nareni groaned. "How many times have I talked to you about this?"

Slav snorted and turned away. He leaned again against the rectangular tower on the town wall where he'd been leaning when Nareni entered. Nareni continued. She looked at Slav with her head tilted forwards and her eyes peering over the tops of her glasses.

"Everyone knows we can't work out our issues with the dead, but we can give them some sort of...meaning. That's what we get when we watch the Necromancer's games. They're violent and twisted...all the dismemberment, the calculated moves....and its true, it's all for entertainment, but without the games the deaths of the dead would feel too hollow"

"And you don't find it sad that we can think of no way of honouring our dead other than mutilating them for spectacle until they crumble?"

Nareni remained silent. She kept her eyes on Slav.

"You don't find it sick, what they've all subscribed to, what they're watching right now?"

Nareni shrugged. "No, not really." She smiled. "I find it kind of exciting, actually, and you know, it's good both ways. You can take pride in the sacrifice of your loved ones, or enjoy the second death of your enemies, your choice, so it is really win-win."

Slav winced.

Nareni laughed.

"Then I guess I'm just the crazy one," Slav said while looking out towards the square graveyard by the grove of Douglas fir trees.

Nareni nodded. "Yup, I guess so." She kept up her smile.

"But you'll gladly end this if it puts away any woman who dies with unfinished feelings for your husband?"

Nareni's face darkened as her expression fell into neutrality.

"Listen, I'm sorry for how bitterly...personal that was, just...god, have you ever believed something alone? I'd kill enjoy the games between the Necromancers, with our dead as their pieces, but I can't, I just can't."

Nareni looked at him more softly. "We'll just have to accept each other for now, and meet where we have common ground. What equipment still needs setting?"

"Nothing...now," said Slav. "I wired it all when everyone was distracted by the first match tonight."

"Then there's nothing for me to help with?" Nareni said.

"Oh no...there still is. Blowing it all to hell is preferable to desecrating the bodies, but it means nothing unless the town can honor them in another way." Slav pulled a ribbon-tied scroll of beige parchment out of his long coat and handed it to Nareni. She took it, tugged an end of the ribbon until it came undone, and flattened out the scroll with both hands. On it she saw a grid of names written in cursive with ink. Above each name sat a small, black, crudely-drawn diagram and detailed sets of coordinates. She looked up at Slav.

"I can work with this," she said, "and make a tribute map of the Zeta cemetery. We can put it up somewhere in town, under glass, I don't know. They'll accept it, in time, with no other option, but they won't see it your way. I don't think the surviving townsfolk ever will understand your sabotage, if I'm being honest; they'll only be forced to accept it, like I said, with no other option really."

Slav kept staring ahead towards the nighttime graveyard he'd wired with dynamite.

"They may be in the dark now," he said, "but they'll get better in time." Slav nodded.

Nareni chortled. She sighed. "I still want to help, but you need to understand, this is why they don't like you, and never will." She kept up a smile while she looked at him from the angle of her tilted head. "You can't judge them by whether or not they support you."

Slav turned just his head halfway towards her.

"So what remains to do?" Nareni said.

"Just to hit the detonator."

"Huh," said Nareni. She listened to the distant commotion of the continuing Necromancer matches and the silence on the opposite side of the town where she and Slav stood. "I thought I'd feel different, being in league with you right before you hit the last cemetery."

"That's the part that keeps most people in line," Slav said. "When they realize that no one is there to stop them from stepping out."

"Where will you be when you detonate it?"

"I can't be in the city when it happens." Slav shivered and calmed his shoulders. "I'll be by the Zeta cemetery near the grove of adjacent trees for cover. I need to be sure the charges go off."

CHAPTER IV

"...Our mayor declared psychological necromancy–or the resurrection of dead, forgotten thoughts–outlawed after three quarters of our town died while lost in 'The Singular Revelation' brought forth by the probing of our memories, lost in the hopeless, colourless, filthy glaucoma which settled over each of our perceptions. Everyone rushed for the town walls, and the first to jump shocked the remaining fourth of us out of the Revelation's effects. We buried our dead in thirty different cemeteries outside the city walls, overwhelming the far fewer graves occupied by natural deaths..."

***

Slav crouched on the far side of the Douglas fir trees clustered on one side of the Zeta Cemetery. Moonlight streamed through the branches but he could not see between their trunks. He lay flat on the ground and covered his head. Slav looked at his watch. It read 5:00 a.m. By now most of the spectators from the Necromancy matches would be in bed.

He pressed the button on the detonator in his right hand.

A thick, almost subsonic roar tore through the earth and shook the ground under Slav. He felt its vibrations in his chest. The dynamite he'd wired together and planted above the graves exploded and kicked up geysers of sprouting dirt, as if the soil rejected that which had been buried six feet into its depths with a violent expulsion. The charges tore through the thin, wooden coffins and ripped the remains therein apart into rubble. Debris whipped through the air. Many pieces bounced off the trees and fell to the ground. Some rained down on the back of Slav's coat. The blast subsided. Slav ran around the grove of trees and took up an observation position from which he could clearly see the town. He removed an eyeglass out of the pouch on his belt. He trained its lens over the stone walls lit up by spotlights.

Slav saw townspeople gathering between the square towers evenly spread along the wall. He could not make an accurate guess as to how many citizens stood there because of the deep night sky.

Slav stayed in the camouflaged tent he set up in the cluster of Douglas firs for the duration of the next day. He waited for a party of people to investigate the remains of the Zeta cemetery, as he expected, but none came forth from the city gates.

He didn't sleep.

CHAPTER V

"...Some school children were the first ones who saw the Necromancers. They saw both of them from their classroom window near the town's border. The students looked through the dirty glass pane and over the town wall six feet away. They saw the young Necromancer with blue lips, a beard, and a black suit, walking with the older one who wore a wide-brimmed hat and a breathing mask. They walked among the tombstones in the Ah Graveyard, where we'd finished burying the last of the Revelation's victims during the previous day. We didn't know who these two men were or what they could accomplish until we saw them make lush grass grow in mere seconds through the fresh dirt we'd packed down over the coffins the day before. More townspeople came forth to view this miraculous regeneration..."

***

Nareni, wrapped in a plaid blanket secured about her collar with a silver brooch, rushed down the gradually declining ground towards Slav's position when the following night fell. She arrived at the grove of trees and marched through it with large steps. She found Slav's tent. When she unzipped the flap she saw nothing inside.

"Why didn't you watch any of the matches last night?" she said out loud.

"Because they're like mechanical chess players," Nareni heard a voice say nearby.

Slav stepped out from behind the trunk of a particularly wide tree.

"You're still here?" Nareni said.

"Why haven't they come yet?" Slav asked.

"I have no idea. When I got back to my apartment no one was around, not even Scott. I saw many down in the plaza by the Mayor's mansion, but I didn't want to join late; they might've suspected something."

Slav walked to the edge of the Douglas firs and looked up the hill towards the town. He kept his hands in his pocket. Nareni saw him lean forward. Slav still wore his reflective sunglasses, but she could tell he squinted by the way lines formed on his face. He turned and walked hurriedly back into the cluster of trees.

"What is it?" Nareni said.

"I saw the closest gate open," he said. "They're sending someone."

"Do you have time to get a head start on them? You can't be here when they arrive. They'll know you did it…"

"I'm not leaving," he said.

Nareni's mouth dropped open and her eyebrows slanted upwards over her nose. "That's insane," she said.

"They have to know why; otherwise, who knows what they'll say about me after I leave."

"You think you can convince them? Do you think they'll really be willing to listen, after you've blown one of the cemeteries apart?"

Slav stepped closer to Nareni. "There's nothing to convince them of! They just need to know my reasons, I don't give a damn what they think beyond that."

Nareni stayed silent for a moment before she said "sure you give a damn."

Slav shrugged. "Believe whatever you want."

"So that's your whole plan, to just explain to whoever comes out why you desecrated their dead, and then what?"

"Hold on a second," Slav said. He shook his head. "You were fine helping me put this plan into action last night, for your own purposes, so where do you get off now being so weepy about the state of the dead?"

Slav sighed. He shook his head. "This isn't the time," he said. "They'll be here soon. You're the one who should be leaving."

"No," Nareni said. "I've been alive here almost twice as long as you have, and you don't have a monopoly on voicing views. You have your reasons you want known, and I have mine."

Slav looked at her and half smiled.

Nareni turned towards the town.

"I want them to know that even an exception has an impact," she said.

"We can tell them soon," said Slav, but after a few more tense minutes of waiting, the townsfolk Slav had seen emerging from the city gates hadn't yet arrived. Slav crouched and moved to the edge of the trees. He saw the column of citizens moving slowly down a dirt road. He saw them halfway between the town and the Douglas fir grove. Slav took his eyeglass out of its pouch and trained it on the advancing group, which he saw consisted of only the town's most elderly residents. They walked along the road single file. Each of them held a pale lantern. The old men wore trousers, collarless shirts, and suspenders. The old women wore nightgowns, their slippers, and shawls over their shoulders.

Nareni had crept up close to Slav.

"What is it?" she said.

Slav exhaled and raised his eyebrows.

"There's a line of the town's elderly coming down the road."

"What?" said Nareni

"That's what I said," said Slav. "I can't make sense of it, but it doesn't change anything, I suppose."

Slav and Nareni stayed out of sight while they silently awaited the group from town's arrival.

The group of about two and a half dozen of the town's most senior residents arrived at the patch of upturned dirt and shattered stone where the Zeta cemetery once stood. They all reached the gravesite together. Their lanterns collectively gave the area a pale, purple glow under the night sky.

They all slowly spun about in a daze. They gazed at the blank wreck of once sacred ground beneath them. Their mouths moved without forming words. They ceased their stunned spinning when they saw Slav and Nareni—who had emerged from the grove of trees—standing side by side before them.

Mr. Dalton stood hunched over on his cane. "Young man," he said, raising one finger slowly towards Slav, "what have you done here?"

"Well this is just horrendous to see," said Ms. Jarvis whose white hair bobbed above her shoulders.

Mr. Sinclair emitted an exaggerated groan as he leaned over, placed his lantern on the ground, and stood up straight again. He stuck his thumbs in the belt loops of his trousers. "Would either of you please care to explain why you robbed the families who had dead here of closure and soothing? Hmmm?"

"You know, I'd really love to beat that smug superiority out of you right here," Slav said, but Nareni placed her hand on his shoulder.

"Slav, please," she whispered before addressing the town's elderly. "We did not rob you of closure, or of being able to grieve," she said as she pulled the grave map Slav had made of the cemetery from the bag slung over her shoulder. "This is exactly as they all were. You know of my skills with design, I can make this into a beautiful memorial plaque for the city, and we can all remember those we've lost, and those who died in the Singular Revelation, but without resorting to all this…madness with dark magic."

Slav slapped his hands together in front of him and shook them up and down for emphasis while he spoke.

"Don't any of you see?" he said. "We can move on now, with dignity! All you've been doing is humiliating these dead…and all I've done is remove their empty bodies from this plain, but not your memory, not from mind, I haven't done that. I never insulted the memories of these dead by toying with them. For twenty-nine years I sat by and watched the annual games between the Necromancers make a mockery of our dead, but I couldn't stand by and see such…such disrespect again, not even one last time…I don't care about your forgiveness, but I need you to understand." Slav exhaled heavily after he finished speaking. His shoulders sagged.

Nareni jumped in before any of the town's elders could respond. "And have you all forgotten how each year's games bring up dead who the Necromancers can't control, who creep into town and haunt those who knew them in life? Is the effect they bring worth it? Is the anxiety of waiting for them worth it? Do you remember how we found Ms. Veneer a year ago after her son's reanimated body sought her out? Or the scene we discovered two years ago in the Sappo Chapel after two resurrected members of the congregation returned to their parish?"

The wind rustled through the high tops of the trees that swayed against the evening. Under the moonlight, the shadows of the branches lashed over the ruined gravesite lit up with the dull purple glow of the townsfolk's handheld lanterns.

Mr. Sinclair let an exaggerated frown fall over his face. He said "Mr. Dalton here has had a very hard life. You two don't want him to find some joy and release, at all?" Mr. Sinclair shook his head.

"You keep saying that," Slav said. "What release?"

"His family has always had it tough in this town, and yet, even though he's the last of them he doesn't feel any of the pain and humiliation from that reputation, not when his deceased relatives rise again each year and triumph in whatever matches they're resurrected for."

"And the Necromancer games are so soothing," said Ms. Jarvis. "You have two sides, you have a lovely nighttime view, a comfortable seat, and you can safely see history sort itself out. Don't you think it's a comfort to witness it all from the town walls, all that death turning back into life, for one evening, especially after what that awful Revelation did to this place?" Ms. Jarvis sighed. She raised her head and spoke again. "And it takes such effort for those nice Necromancer boys to do what they do for us, they've spent a full twenty-nine years working towards this goal, a clean sweep of the thirty cemeteries, giving closure to the families who have dead in each one, and now, thanks to you two, some will never get their closure. It's a shame..."

Nareni looked among the elderly gathered around her and Slav in the remains of the destroyed graveyard. She said "what closure? Did they not receive enough at the funerals?"

Despite his hunched over posture, Mr. Dalton lifted his cane and pointed it at Slav as he spoke. "Your problem is that you haven't thought of the old feuds."

"The old feuds?" Slav said.

"That's right," said Mr. Sinclair. "Didn't think of that did you? Old, unfinished quarrels once embroiled this town. You know we can't resolve our issues with the dead, or their issues with us. A disagreement between two families would begin, those who began it would die in the fight, and their descendants would carry on the conflict, demanding satisfaction, as the families of the other dead also demanded, and it would go on..."

"Until the web of feuds in this town got so convoluted," Ms. Jarvis continued, "that no one could find a path back to peace, no one could remember one..."

Mr. Dalton almost spoke, but he, Mr. Sinclair, and Ms. Jarvis became suddenly quiet.

Slav looked among them. "Is that when the town decided to the resurrect memories of its citizens with psychological necromancy? Was it originally an attempt to sort out which feuds began where?"

Mr. Dalton looked at the ground. Ms. Jarvis kept her lips sealed but nodded once while her eyes became wet with tears.

Nareni sneered as she also looked among Mr. Dalton, Mr. Sinclar, Ms. Jarvis, and the rest of the town's most elderly residents gathered around them.

"And that's why the Singular Revelation took over the minds of the town's residents and drove them over the walls?" she said.

"Don't be so dismissive, dear," said Ms. Jarvis. "I felt it to be a tragedy too, all those citizens suddenly gone, all their business left unfinished...until those two nice Necromancers came along."

Slav didn't look at the crowd around him in the cemetery. He kept looking towards the city walls from behind his reflective glasses. "And that's why the betting rings sprung up around the matches." he said.

"Precisely!" said Mr. Sinclair, stepping forward and nodding. "We bet on the resurrected dead, because only their performance in the games can settle who is worthy of respect, or who was strongest..."

"Or fastest..." Mr. Dalton said.

"Or which family should prevail in an ongoing dispute,"

said Ms. Jarvis.

"Twenty-nine years," Mr. Sinclair said. "Twenty-nine matches…with only one more to go next year before we've finished exhuming the dead and sorting out their troublesome legacies among us…but you've both prevented that process from ever being completed." Mr. Sinclair put his hands in his pockets. "Anyone who had dead in the Zeta cemetery will never have their unsolved business settled. Those families are never going to get a chance at one final, vicarious glory through their resurrected dead, thanks to both of you." Mr. Sinclair kicked a broken piece of tombstone half-sticking out of the dirt. The jagged section of granite skidded over to Slav's feet.

Slav kicked the stone back.

"And you really think that if all thirty cemeteries worth of dead had been resurrected, toyed with, and turned into dust, that conflicts in town would be permanently solved?" he said. "If I hadn't destroyed this cemetery, what would you have done after the last Necromancy match, after the last of the dead had been used up? There aren't enough natural deaths a year here to keep up these yearly games." Slav turned towards Mr. Sinclair. "Didn't think of that, did you? You'd be in the exact same situation as you are now, only a year later. Face it, the Necromancy matches were going to end anyway once all this town's dead were used up and there were no more bodies to raise with only a trickle coming in. There was never any escaping that outcome. Now this town needs to decide how to continue, how to really move on, only without the distraction of digging up the dead and having them play out our problems for some spectacle."

"But you can still honor your dead, you needn't lose your memories of them. Don't you remember how it was before we learned black magic?" Nareni said. She again held up the map of graves in the Zeta cemetery which Slav had made. "I can make this map, and the maps of all the cemeteries, into beautiful, engraved works of art, which we can display around town, we can…" but Nareni stopped when Ms. Jarvis stepped forward with her mouth half open and a smile on her face. Her eyes sparkled in the moonlight and stayed open wide. She gently took the grave map from Nareni's hands.

"May I see this, dear?" she said.

"Of course," said Nareni.

"Oh my," said Ms. Jarvis, who examined the map closely. "This says exactly where all the graves were, each and every position."

"And the exact distances between them," said Slav. "You're welcome."

"I think we can use this," Ms. Jarvis said to all the eldest town residents gathered around her. They moved closer behind Ms. Jarvis and peered at the gravesite map. They turned to each other and nodded while frowning under calm eyes. They broke apart like billiards and spread out across the broken ground of the blown-up cemetery. With the graveyard map as their guide, the most elderly townsfolk each moved to a spot where a coffin had formerly been buried. They stood in a collective grid pattern, all of them facing the brightly lit town walls.

Mr. Sinclair said "you asked what we are to do now that all the town's graveyards have been resurrected and used up into dust…"

"Or blown apart," said Mr. Dalton.

"You'd know what to do if you'd ever worked the old farms," said Mr. Sinclair.

Slav and Nareni stood among the old townspeople standing on former gravesites. They said nothing. The wind intensified above them all and bristled hard through the tops of the Douglas firs.

Ms. Jarvis smiled. "My dear, after the harvest has been reaped…you replant," she said.

Each of the town's eldest citizens simultaneously pulled pocket knives out from their pockets or purses and crudely slashed their own throats. They each collapsed into a heap atop a spot in the broken soil where graves had formerly been laid. They all fell at once. The blood spitting and trickling forth from their torn jugulars soaked into the dirt under their bodies.

Mr. Dalton's bony hand still clutched the curved grip of his cane. Mr. Sinclair still had one hand in a pocket. Ms. Jarvis maintained her posture after she cut her own throat. She'd clasped her hands against her stomach and lowered herself onto her knees in the dirt. She fell forwards. She lay out straight on her front with her hands beneath her and her face burrowed into the soil. The rest of the elderly bodies lay in a variety of positions.

Slav's mouth hung half open, but his eyes remained stoic behind mirrored lenses. Nareni looked around with an expression of stunned horror behind her thick glasses.

After the bodies fell, Slav and Nareni saw both Necromancers standing on the far side of the cemetery.

The Necromancer wearing glasses, a wide-brimmed leather hat, and a large air-filtration mask began walking among the freshly lifeless bodies lying in rows before him. The Necromancer with blue lips and a long beard wearing a black suit and turtleneck stayed still. He began rolling a cigarette, tapping out tobacco from a small pouch.

Nareni stayed still where she stood. "Next year you'll raise this batch of dead to use in more Necromancy games between you two for the town, won't you?" she said before stopping.

"And the next eldest citizens will plant themselves for the following year," Slav said before rolling his head and turning away momentarily.

Both Necromancers said nothing.

"You mean me to believe you can't summon even a word?" said Nareni.

26

The one wearing an air-filtration mask stopped and turned towards her. He raised his gloved hands. He spoke, and his voice came out hollow and distorted through his mask.

"Madame," he said, "I do not see how their actions are connected to me."

"You see," said the other Necromancer who placed his rolled cigarette between his blue lips and lit it with a match. He held it between the index and middle fingers on one of his rough hands. He raised his eyebrows in an expression of alarm whenever he spoke. "This is what we do, were all shaping the world with everything we do, right?" he made a wide circular motion with his unoccupied hand. "And this is what we do…now we can't help that," he placed his free hand on his chest and shook his head, "any more than a Necromancer can help, say, taking action when you think it's necessary, right? That's how were sculpting the world, really, and it's a reflection of ourselves…"

"Just stop," said Slav.

The Necromancer with blue lips and a beard leaned back and narrowed his eyes before turning away. The other one in the large breathing mask finished walking among the rows of newly deceased bodies. He walked back to his partner and stood next to him. The Necromancer in the black suit took a red and gold tube out from inside his jacket. He knelt down and pressed it into the dirt. He lit the wick with the glowing end of his cigarette. A bright red-gold streak flew out of the tube and far into the black sky where it exploded in flowering bursts of its two colours. The fireworks flamed out. Both Necromancers faced the townsfolk atop the city walls and lifted their arms into the air. They stood straight and nodded solemnly before lowering their arms and walking apart in opposite directions.

Slav and Nareni looked towards the rows of townspeople gathered on the town walls as well. The townsfolk began singing after the fireworks burst against the night sky, confirming the planting of the harvest for the following year's matches. The song the townspeople sang stirred inside a low octave. The melody began mournfully but steadily rose according to a slow march into a prideful, muscular song of respectful commemoration

"for the sacrifice, of the eldest folk
to carry on, the graveyard games
like the sweat of sowing seeds
for the sweetest harvest yield."

CHAPTER VI

"...The mayor walked out alone past the town walls and spoke to both Necromancers perusing the Ah Cemetery. Most surviving townsfolk had climbed the walls by then so they could watch this meeting they could not hear. The mayor walked alone back into the city when it finished.

He called the population to the square plaza outside his mansion. We learned of the Necromancers' offer to resurrect the jubilant moods and optimistic thinking which the depression from the Singular Revelation had stolen from our minds. But we recoiled into silence when we heard this suggestion, fearing that a mental torture worse than the Revelation might result from a re-engagement with psychological necromancy.

Several people looked away and shuffled their feet, until our Mayor presented us with the second option of letting the Necromancers resurrect just the physical forms of our dead to participate in their games, which the two strangers said they'd play out in each of our cemeteries. It gave us townsfolk an unnatural spectacle larger than ourselves and powerful enough to entrance our dampened minds.

In it, The Necromancers said, we'd find closure in our

dead's sacred, utilitarian new purpose, as well as from the selection of vicarious emotions that arise from the drama of battle. We'd find glory in the victories of our loved ones, they said, and fulfillment in the deaths of our enemies, so none would feel deprived or unsatisfied when all the resurrected corpses crumbled into dust after the employed necromancy spells wore off.

Many of us grumbled unhappily, but the crowd dispersed without incident. That night, one by one, the citizens of the town gathered on the wall looking out over the Ah Cemetery and watched the Necromancers play their first matches with our dead.

Even more spectators came out a year later for the second set of matches at the Beh Cemetery, and the audience size for all subsequent yearly matches held steady, because each post-match morning found a town populace moving through their daily activities with renewed vigor in anticipation of the cathartic thrills awaiting them after nightfall one night a year..."

Slav and Nareni walked in silence back to Slav's encampment on the other side of the nearby grove of trees. As Slav marched about, gathering up supplies and taking down his tent, Nareni waited for him to speak, but he said nothing.

Finally, Nareni said "what are you going to do now? Looks like they aren't punishing you."

"There's no point to punishing me; I had not effect, I did nothing, basically."

"I'm sorry," Nareni said.

"No, I'm sorry for you," said Slav. "And for anyone who gets a visit from the resurrected." Slav looked away from Nareni. "And I'm sorry if any of Scott's other 'lapses' come back." Slav winced, expecting the hurtful impact of his reminder to spread over Nareni's face. When he brought himself to look her in the eye he saw her tearing up, but she stood straight and did not quiver. She stepped forward and hugged Slav. He returned her embrace and let her tears run over the fabric of his coat. When she stepped back from him she said, "there won't be any more," as she wiped her cheek with the back of her hand, "I'm not going to be with him after this morning."

Slav pursed his lips and looked down. "I understand," he said.

"Are you still going to leave?" said Nareni.

"Yes," said Slav. "I can't be part of the town if the Necromancy games have to continue, I wish I could, I do."

"I know," said Nareni, "I understand."

"I'm okay with it, though, strangely," Slav said. "I know my view on the matches is an...exception in this town, I guess."

"Exactly," said Nareni as she smiled politely.

Slav slung the straps of his pack over his shoulders. He nodded in absent minded agreement before adding "outliers among the living, outliers among the dead." He laughed. "Thank you for your help, by the way."

"Thank you for the map of the grave. I'm still going to use it."

"I'm glad," said Slav before he waved and turned away. He followed one of the dirt roads leading down the sloping ground away from the town. Nareni walked back to town along the same path in the opposite, uphill direction.

***

A farmer drives his red tractor between the stalks of corn growing in rows on his farm during a hot July morning several years later. Some husks are green, but the vast majority are tan coloured and dry. The large black tires roll over the long, broken grass pressed into the ground. Select bits of it stay stuck to the tires as they rotate. The farmer doesn't smile. He wears a hat with a short brim pulled down to his brow. His hands rest on top of the large steering wheel in front of him. His body bounces as the tractor lurches along. Among this particular section of his crops he can't see the town walls far to his right.

When he reaches the wooden fence signaling the end of this field, as well as his property, he turns his tractor, intending to drive back down the next row of crops. He puts his foot on the brakes after he turns though, and looks over the fence at the fields next to his own.

They belong to the new Effe cemetery.

The farmer sees a cemetery worker driving a ride-on lawn mower over the grass between the tombstones. She reaches the end of the graveyard's property and turns, intending to drive back down the next row of graves. She waves to the corn farmer as she passes by her side of the wooden fence.

The farmer nods, but doesn't wave back, for he refuses to call the cemetery workers farmers, as most of the town does, even if what they plant in the ground is eventually brought out of the earth—once a year—for a purpose essential to the town's existence.

THE END

ABOUT THE AUTHOR

PAUL EDWARD COSTA

Paul is a writer and spoken word performer who has published fiction, non-fiction, and poetry in "Timber Journal", "Entropy", "Thrice Fiction", "Emerge Literary Journal", "The J.J. Outre Review", "The Eunoia Review", "Songs of Eretz Poetry Review", "Alien Mouth", "The Bookends Review", "REAL: Regarding Arts and Letters", and other periodicals. He is the founder of the ongoing "Paul's Poetry Night" spoken word series in the Greater Toronto Area. Paul earned a Specialized Honors BA in History and a BA in Education at York University. He is also a high school English teacher with the Peel District School Board.

SOCIAL MEDIA:
Facebook: https://m.facebook.com/PaulEdwardCosta/
YouTube: https://www.youtube.com/PaulEdwardCosta
Instagram: https://www.instagram.com/paul.edward.costa/
Amazon.com: https://www.amazon.com/Paul-Edward-Costa/e/B01NA0BTR9/
Twitter: @paul_e_costa